For Ann and Sara

Little, Brown and Company

Hachette Book Group
237 Park Avenue, New York, NY 10017
Visit our website at www.lb-kids.com

Little, Brown and Company is a division of Hachette Book Group, Inc.
The Little, Brown name and logo are trademarks of Hachette Book Group, Inc.

The publisher is not responsible for websites (or their content) that are not owned by the publisher.

First Edition: May 2006

Library of Congress Cataloging-in-Publication Data

Gall, Chris.
Dear fish / written and illustrated by Chris Gall. — 1st ed.
p. cm.
Summary: One afternoon at the beach, a small boy puts an invitation to the fish to come for a visit in a bottle and throws it into the ocean, and the results are unprecedented.
ISBN 978-0-316-05847-6
[1. Beach — Fiction.   2. Ocean — Fiction.   3. Fish — Fiction.   4. Humorous stories.]   I. Title.
PZ7.G1352De 2005
[E] — dc22

2005003828

10 9 8 7 6 5 4 3 2

SC

Manufactured in China

The illustrations for this book were done by hand engraving clay-coated board
and then digitizing with Adobe Illustrator for adjustments and color.
The text was set in OldClaude, and the display type was hand-lettered.

Dear Fish

written and illustrated by

CHRIS GALL

LITTLE, BROWN AND COMPANY
New York Boston

Peter Alan and his family had never seen a finer day at the beach. Ocean breezes rippled through their umbrella, clouds skipped carefree overhead, and even the seagulls were on their best behavior. (Which was asking a lot of a seagull.)

Peter Alan spent most of the day leaping over tide pools, peeking under rocks, and wondering what kinds of curious creatures might live beneath the swirling water.

Peter Alan had an idea. He ran back to the blanket, found a pencil and paper, and began to write:

Dear Fish,
Where you live is pretty cool. You should come visit us someday. Plus my Mom makes good pies.
Sincerely,
Peter Alan

He pushed the note into an empty bottle, screwed the cap on tight, and threw it as far as he could into the churning sea.

After all the chips had been eaten, the castles made, the shells collected, and the sun had dissolved into the sea, Peter Alan's family packed up and headed home.

The next morning, while Peter Alan was getting ready for school, he heard

a strange dripping and

a flipping,

a flopping and

a gurgling.

And a strong smell was coming from behind the shower curtain. . . .

ext door, Mr. Adams was getting ready to mow his lawn. From the other side of his fence he heard a peculiar

chomping and

a slurping,

a gnawing and

a burping.

Then a whole family of very startled mice leapt out from under the leaves and dashed away.

Down the street at Sally's house, even stranger things were going on. Sally was looking for some balloons for her birthday party, and luckily she found some funny (but rather smelly) ones in a closet. Just as the party was about to start, she heard

a *crash*,

a *smash*,

a *wiggling* and

a *jiggling*,

and a deep bellowing overhead that shook the entire house. . . .

Down at the ballpark, it was the bottom of the ninth inning. Without looking, Casey McGraw grabbed a bat from the dugout and ran to the plate. The crowd hushed as he swung with all his might. And with

a *smack*,

a *crunch*,

a *munch* and

a *gulp*,

the game was over.

Outside of town at the rodeo, Cole Trenton (the roughest, toughest, stinkiest cowboy that ever rode a steer) climbed onto a creature that he'd heard just couldn't be ridden. Though he

yanked and **yelled** and **spurred** and **spat**,

Cole was later found two counties away.

Meanwhile, Peter Alan's dad was building a tree house. But before he could reach for his saw, he felt a great

swooping and

whooshing and

a hammering and

yammering.

Then he was left in a cloud of sawdust.

Downtown at the beauty parlor, Peter Alan's mom had just leaned back to enjoy the

combing and

curling and

snipping and

spraying.

Until she felt something clammy and wet stick to her cheek.

Just at that moment, Mrs. Adams burst through the door and exclaimed, "There's something going on at the school!"

Peter Alan returned from school that afternoon feeling more than a little slimy. This was more of a visit than Peter Alan had expected. He wrote another note:

Dear Fish,
Thank you for coming to see us. You are nice, but you are fish. You should live at home. Plus I think I hear your mothers calling you.
Sincerely,
Peter Alan

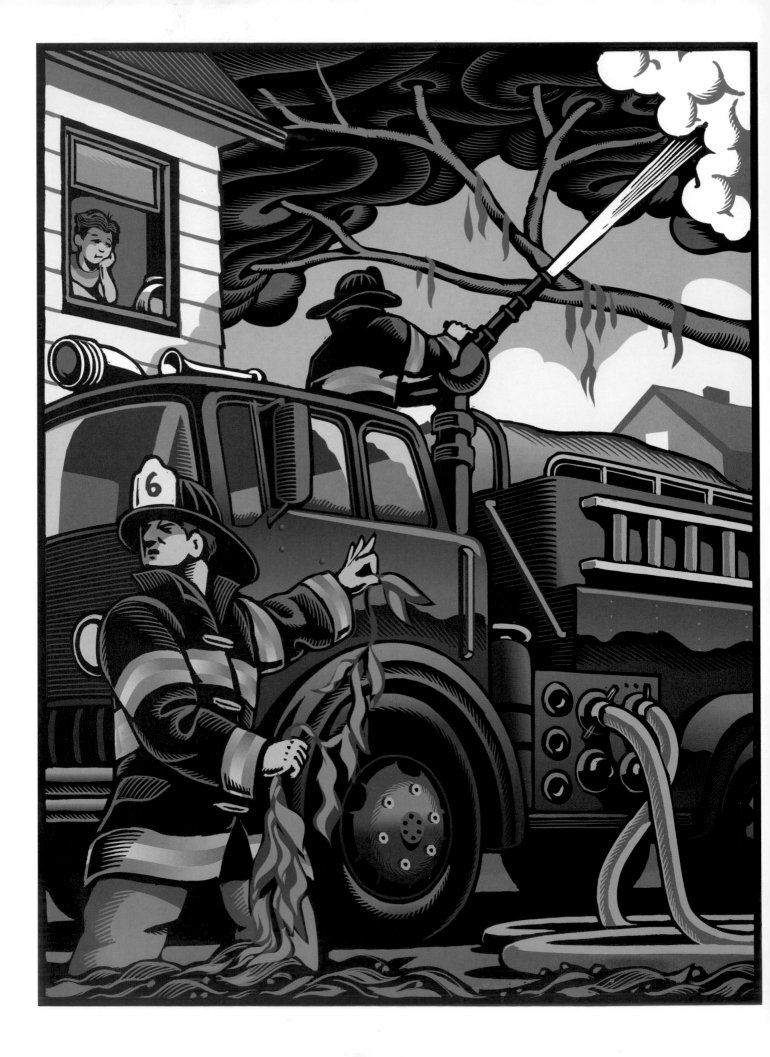

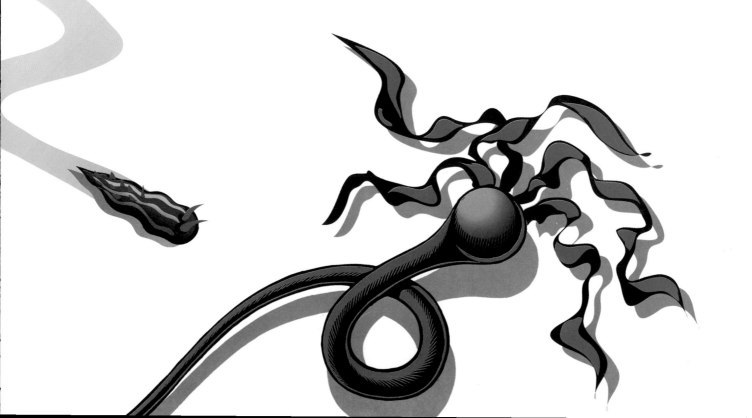

everal weeks later, the fishy smells finally started to fade. The firemen had gotten the fish goo out of the trees. The police had removed most of the shark eggs from the fountain in the town square. The town was nearly cleaned up (except for the stains left behind by the sea slugs—you can never get those out).

And Peter Alan was finally allowed to have goldfish in his room again, but he had to promise never to speak to them, write to them, or signal them in any way.

ater that summer the family decided it was safe to return to the beach. Peter Alan promised not to throw any more trash into the ocean and to stay away from the tide pools. So he spent his day climbing on rocks, inspecting seaweed, and keeping a sharp lookout for pirates. Until . . .

On a small sliver of sand by the water's edge, down deep in the rocks, something caught Peter Alan's eye. There seemed to be something inside. . . .

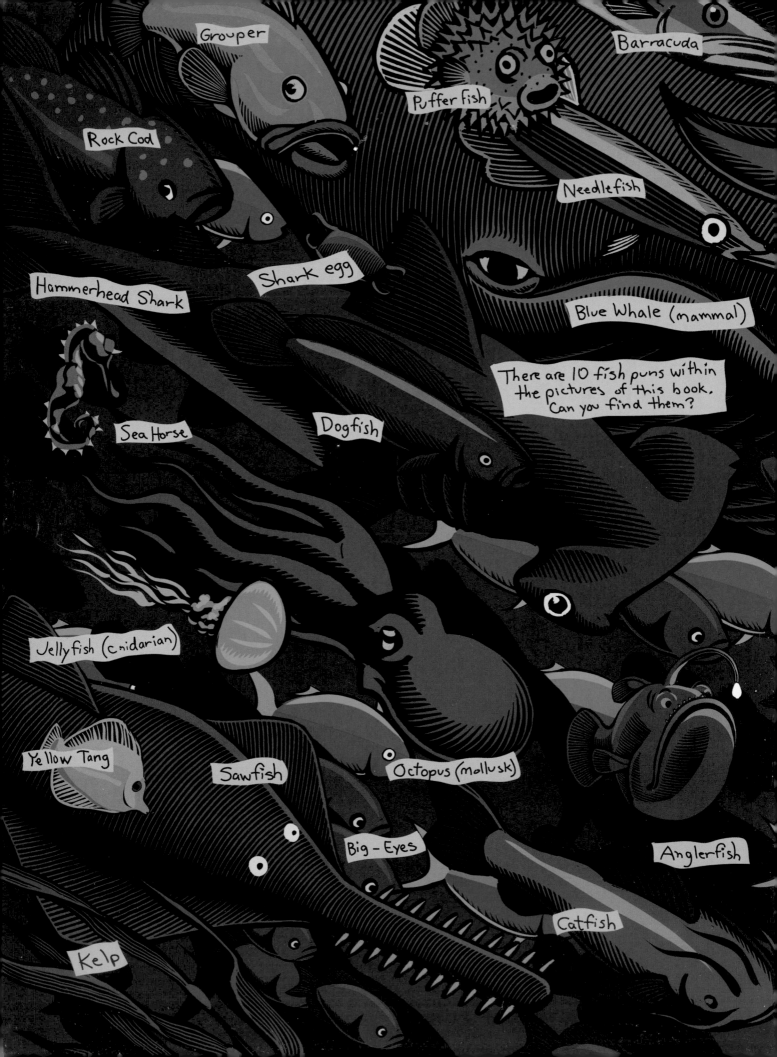